TEEN PROBLEMS

TEENS AND CYBERBULLYING

By Marie-Thérèse Miller, PhD

ReferencePoint Press®

San Diego, CA

ReferencePoint Press®

Printed in the United States

For more information, contact:
ReferencePoint Press, Inc.
PO Box 27779
San Diego, CA 92198
www.ReferencePointPress.com

Content Consultant: Jack Rivituso, Ed.D., Professor of Cybersecurity & Information Technology, SUNY Cobleskill

LIBRARY OF CONGRESS CATALOGING-IN-PUBLICATION DATA

Names: Miller, Marie-Therese, author.
Title: Teens and cyberbullying / by Marie-Thérèse Miller, PhD.
Description: San Diego : ReferencePoint Press, 2021. | Series: Teen problems | Includes bibliographical references and index. | Audience: Grades 10-12
Identifiers: LCCN 2020003709 (print) | LCCN 2020003710 (eBook) | ISBN 9781682829615 (hardcover) | ISBN 9781682829622 (eBook)
Subjects: LCSH: Cyberbullying--Juvenile literature. | Computer crimes--Juvenile literature. | Cyberbullying--Prevention--Juvenile literature.
Classification: LCC HV6773.15.C92 M555 2021 (print) | LCC HV6773.15.C92 (eBook) | DDC 302.34/3--dc23
LC record available at https://lccn.loc.gov/2020003709
LC eBook record available at https://lccn.loc.gov/2020003710

CONTENTS

INTRODUCTION

TRIUMPH OVER CYBERBULLYING

Lizzie Velásquez was born with Marfanoid-progeroid-lipodystrophy syndrome. The syndrome affects her outward appearance and keeps her from gaining weight. In addition, Velásquez has impaired vision. Because of her outward appearance, she was the target of bullying. When Velásquez was a student in grade school, she was ignored and isolated. She said, "I remember going up to groups of kids that were playing and they would just walk away as if I wasn't there."[1] Classmates also made mean remarks about the way she looked.

Eventually, Velásquez decided to introduce herself to her class at the start of each school year. This way, she could explain her syndrome to her classmates so they would understand. The approach was effective for those in her class. However, the bullying continued outside the classroom. Velásquez said, "As soon as we walked out of the classroom

More than 20 percent of students report that they have been bullied. Cyberbullying has become more common in the twenty-first century.

doors, it was back to the stares, and the points, and the whispers."[2]

In middle school, Velásquez tried out for the cheerleading squad and made it. Overall, things were going better in middle school and high school. However, when Velásquez was seventeen years old, she was a target of cyberbullying. Cyberbullying is bullying through electronic means. She found a

> "They were calling me a monster or asking why my parents didn't abort me."[3]
>
> *—Lizzie Velásquez, anti-cyberbullying advocate, on YouTube commenters*

video of herself on YouTube. It was titled "The World's Ugliest Woman." She was stunned and could not stop herself from reading the hundreds of cruel comments. "They were calling me a monster or asking why my parents didn't abort me," Velásquez said.[3] Some commenters even suggested she kill herself. "I'm pretty sure I cried myself to sleep a few nights after that," she said.[4]

Velásquez contacted YouTube and had the video removed. Then, the person who posted the video contacted her directly. He told her that he would keep posting the video no matter what. Velásquez's sadness turned to anger. She became determined to do something about cyberbullying.

A few years later, Velásquez began her own YouTube channel. On the channel, she spoke out against cyberbullying and encouraged people to spread love and positivity on the internet. She does not block people from her channel because she believes that what she says is for those who bully as well as for those who are the targets of bullying. She said, "I don't block anybody. I do it for the bullies too. As my dad always says, they might be going through something worse than what I'm going through."[5]

Lizzie Velásquez has a condition that prevents her from gaining weight. She became an advocate against cyberbullying after people bullied her for her appearance.

Velásquez took her experiences with bullying and cyberbullying and used them as motivation to make a difference. She gave a talk that was viewed by millions of people. She has written inspirational books and given motivational speeches all

According to a survey by i-Safe America, nearly 50 percent of kids reported being victims of cyberbullying. A similar percentage admitted to cyberbullying others.

over the world. She has advocated for the passage of the Safe Schools Improvement Act in Washington, DC, which is a federal bill that would require schools to address bullying. The bill was still pending in March 2020. Velásquez wanted to continue her advocacy. She said, "My plan is to work as hard as my little body will work with me so that I can help make the amazing, incredible place that we call the internet a happier, more supportive, and more positive community for all of us to hang out."[6]

> "My plan is to work as hard as my little body will work with me so that I can help make the amazing, incredible place that we call the internet a happier, more supportive, and more positive community for all of us to hang out."[6]
>
> *—Lizzie Velásquez, anti-cyberbullying advocate*

Cyberbullying causes pain and sadness to the victims. Velásquez was able to overcome her experience with cyberbullying and create a meaningful path for herself. Not everyone who is cyberbullied has such a positive outcome. Cyberbullying can lead to psychological disorders. Those psychological problems can extend into adulthood.

Experts in bullying have studied the effects of cyberbullying on individuals. They have also identified groups in society that are especially vulnerable to cyberbullying. These professionals offer concrete ways to avoid cyberbullying or to deal with it when it happens.

CHAPTER ONE

WHAT IS TEEN CYBERBULLYING?

Teens are active in the digital world. They enthusiastically use devices such as cell phones, computers, tablets, and gaming consoles. Technology has many positives to offer. Teens can text their friends to keep in touch after school or make plans to meet up and do something fun together. The internet makes researching for school projects and papers easier. There are social media sites to share thoughts, news, and funny memes.

CYBERBULLYING DEFINED

Online access also presents challenges. Sometimes, the internet becomes a place to write mean comments or share embarrassing photos or videos. It becomes a way to cyberbully. Cyberbullying happens when an individual or a group uses digital means to intentionally cause repeated harm to another person.

In order to understand cyberbullying, it is important to know exactly what bullying is and what it is not. A person who bullies has the goal of causing physical or psychological pain to

Teenagers spend many hours every day online. While technology allows teens to access information and communicate easily, it also introduces the risk of cyberbullying.

another person. Bullying is an intentional, repeated behavior. One exchange of an unkind word or embarrassing comment does not fit the definition of bullying.

In bullying, there is an actual or perceived power differential. For example, the bully might be physically larger than the victim. There might be a difference in intellectual ability between the bully and victim. The power difference can also be social, in which the person bullying could be more popular than the target.

Professors Sameer Hinduja and Justin W. Patchin write that the difference in power in cyberbullying can be different than in real-world bullying. The power difference could be that the cyberbully is more skilled when it comes to digital media. The cyberbully could have access to private photos or information about the victim that he can share, and that makes him more powerful than the target.

Bullying happens in many places. Teens are often bullied at school. It might also happen off school grounds, such as on the school bus or in the victim's neighborhood. Cyberbullying has a particularly long reach. It can happen anywhere there is a digital connection. With cyberbullying, the bully and victim do not have to be in the same location. Cyberbullying can take place at any time, twenty-four hours a day. Online bullying has an element of permanence. Even if a cruel tweet is deleted, it can remain as a screenshot. Bullying spreads quickly online, such as when embarrassing videos are shared and go viral.

CYBERBULLYING TYPES AND METHODS

There are many types of cyberbullying. These can include gossip, rumor-spreading, cruel comments, threats, embarrassment, and exclusion. And there are many ways that cyberbullying can occur. With a cell phone, a person can relay cruel or threatening communications by calling, leaving

PREVALENCE OF CYBERBULLYING

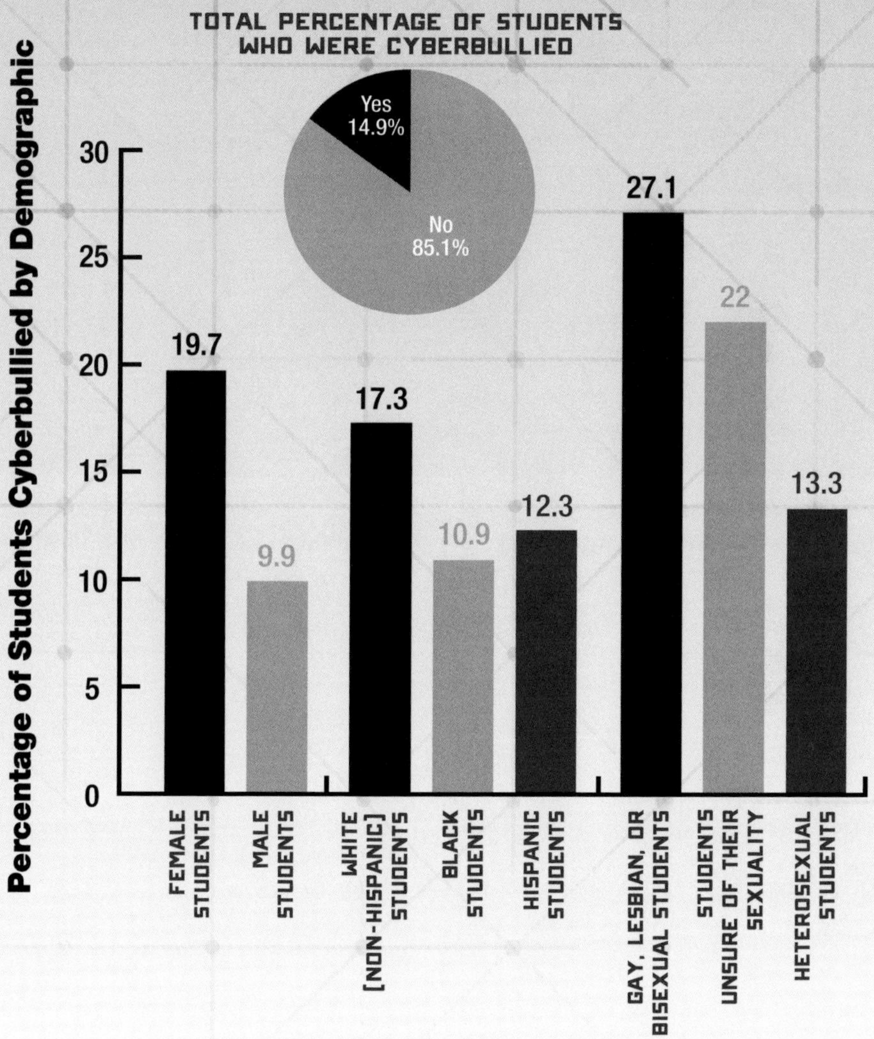

Source: Laura Kann, Tim McManus, William Harris, et al., "Youth Risk Behavior Surveillance—United States, 2017," Surveillance Summaries, *June 15, 2018. www.cdc.gov.*

The 2017 Youth Risk Behavior Survey (YRBS) asked students in grades nine through twelve if they had been bullied electronically over the last twelve months. The researchers defined electronic bullying as being bullied through texting, Facebook, Instagram, or other social media.

Around half of the victims of cyberbullying do not know the identity of their bully. Cyberbullies can make anonymous comments or create fake profiles.

voice messages, or texting. The bully could also send hurtful messages to the victim through email.

Cyberbullying can also take place on social media platforms, such as Facebook, Instagram, Twitter, or YouTube. Bullies might add mean posts or comments. Cyberbullies could use social media private messaging as well. Embarrassing photos or videos taken of the victim might be shared to these sites.

Sometimes, a bully makes a fake profile to impersonate the victim on social media. She pretends to be the victim and posts comments, photos, or videos. These posts are designed to hurt the victim's reputation. The cyberbully, for instance, could make racist comments from this fake profile. The bully might also create a fake profile to hide herself while she cyberbullies. This is precisely what happened to Megan Meier from Dardenne Prairie, Missouri, in 2006. When Megan was thirteen, her parents let her join the social media platform Myspace. A boy named Josh Evans contacted her. His picture showed a good-looking young man, and he wrote her complimentary messages. Megan had low self-esteem, which means she didn't value herself. Megan welcomed his kind comments.

Suddenly, Josh's comments turned cruel. He wrote, "I don't know if I

ANGER-INDUCING TROLLS AND BOTS

It is important to understand that some people comment on social media just to elicit a reaction. Trolls are people who jump into an online discussion and comment negatively or with outrageous opinions merely to start an argument or make others angry. Experts recommend not responding to trolls.

Bots can also cause trouble online. Bots are automated programs that perform a certain task. On Twitter, there are bots that Tweet political propaganda. If someone is fooled into believing the bots are real people sharing their opinions, that person might get into heated conversations that began with the bot. Bots can infuriate others and turn groups of people against one another.

There are signs that point to a fake social media account or bot. If the profile photo is too perfect or if the profile description is exaggerated, this suggests a fake account or bot. When the account hardly has any followers, but it follows many others, this is another clue.

Whether it is a troll, a bot, or a peer making a person angry online, the best thing to do is walk away from the digital device. That way, people won't make comments they might regret. Their anger may subside in the time they are away.

want to be friends with you anymore because I've heard that you are not very nice to your friends." Others joined in the bullying. Megan saw messages calling her "fat" and "slut." The last thing she read said: "The world would be a better place without you."[7] Megan's mother, Tina Meier, was upset with the vulgar words Megan was writing in response to her bullies. Megan ran to her room. On the way, she saw her father, who tried to calm her. Twenty minutes later, Tina found her. Megan had killed herself.

Six weeks later, it was discovered that Josh Evans didn't exist. Lori Drew, the mother of one of Meier's former friends, had created a fake profile. Drew said she wanted to see what Megan was saying about her daughter, Sarah. Drew, Sarah, and Drew's teen employee had been communicating with Megan as Josh.

Drew was initially convicted of a misdemeanor connected to this cyberbullying incident, but a federal judge overturned the conviction. Tina Meier created the Megan Meier Foundation in her daughter's memory "to support and inspire actions to end bullying, cyberbullying, and suicide."[8]

Another way teens encounter cyberbullying is through online gaming. Consoles such as the Xbox and PlayStation allow users to speak to other players through headsets. But cyberbullies can say unkind things while playing. Sometimes, the bully convinces others to exclude the victim from games. The cyberbully may also start a rumor that the victim isn't any good at the game.

Many online games allow players to create their own avatars and alter egos. Groups of anonymous players may gang up against another user and exclude that player from the game.

Exclusion is a form of social bullying found both in cyberspace and in person. It isolates the victim and can cause psychological damage. In fact, some societies use exclusion as a form of severe punishment. Author Nancy E. Willard writes, "Recall that in many tribal societies, exclusion of a member is considered an extremely harsh punishment. Likewise, excommunication from a religious community is considered the ultimate punishment."[9] Exclusion can cause a teen major distress. When done with the intent to harm, social exclusion is considered a form of bullying.

Some cyberbullies use digital means to share the personal information of a victim. The target's telephone number and address might be released, for example. The act of finding and publishing private information is known as doxxing. This information is then used to harass the victim.

CHARACTERISTICS OF VICTIMS AND BULLIES

Experts have noted particular characteristics associated with victims and bullies. Those at risk to be targeted by bullies are often people who are perceived as different. They might be gifted intellectually, or they might have learning disabilities. The victim might look physically different. She could be heavier or slimmer than others. He could be shorter or taller than others.

The book *Bully: An Action Plan for Teachers, Parents, and Communities to Combat the Bullying Crisis* is a companion to the 2011 documentary film *Bully*. The book lists people who might be perceived as different and therefore at risk for being bullied. This includes "children stereotyped by cultural bias, including ethnicity and religious factors; children labeled with a sexual identity (gay, lesbian, bisexual, transgender youth); [and] children who contradict gender stereotypes."[10]

Students who are perceived as being different are often victims of bullying. LGBTQ students face higher instances of bullying than non-LGBTQ peers.

Frequently, victims are not members of the popular group. They might have few or no friends. With nobody to stick up for them, they are vulnerable to bullying. Bullies view them as unable to defend themselves. Victims might have depression or anxiety. A victim can also have low self-esteem.

Many bullies are confident and popular. They bully to maintain or increase that popularity. Antibullying expert and clinical psychologist Joel Haber says that those who bully "are the kids that everyone sees as leaders, but they are different from leaders in one major way. Leaders have empathy and are inclusive; and bullies do not use their empathy and are exclusive."[11] These bullies lack empathy, the ability to understand the feelings and thoughts of another person.

> "Leaders have empathy and are inclusive; and bullies do not use their empathy and are exclusive."[11]
>
> *—Antibullying expert and clinical psychologist Joel Haber*

Others who bully might be depressed or anxious with low self-esteem. Those who bully often have difficulties in their home lives. They have learned that aggression and violence are acceptable ways to solve problems.

WHY DOES CYBERBULLYING HAPPEN?

Hinduja and Patchin have surveyed nearly 15,000 students from schools all around the United States. They asked those students questions about their experiences with bullying and cyberbullying. Hinduja and Patchin note, "Youth who spent more time online or who were more computer proficient

> "Youth who spent more time online or who were more computer proficient were more likely to experience cyberbullying, both as victims and as bullies."[12]
>
> *—Professors Sameer Hinduja and Justin W. Patchin*

were more likely to experience cyberbullying, both as victims and as bullies."[12]

Cyberbullies do not have to face their victims. Those bullying online can write that someone is a "loser" or "ugly" without seeing the hurt in the victim's eyes. People who bully in cyberspace may lose track of the victim's humanity. Frequently, people who bully online are emboldened because they believe they are acting anonymously. Cyberbullies often don't worry that they will be caught or face any consequences. However, Hinduja and Patchin explain that true anonymity is rare in the digital world. Every digital device is assigned a unique set of numbers known as an Internet Protocol (IP) address when the device is connected to the internet. Data and communications that are sent from that device can be traced back to the IP address. Digital service providers can then connect that address to the person registered to it.

REASONS CYBERBULLYING CONTINUES

Teens who are the targets of cyberbullies are often reluctant to seek help, so the bullying continues. Victims might not share their experiences because they are afraid that they will be blamed. They also worry that their parents will restrict access to their computers or cell phones. Parents might believe that if their teen stopped using all digital devices the cyberbullying

FIGHTING BULLYING WITH THE INTERNET

In September 2019, a fourth-grade student in Florida wanted to participate in his school's college colors day. He did not own a T-shirt from his favorite team, the University of Tennessee Volunteers, so he made his own. He created the university logo on a piece of paper and attached it to an orange T-shirt. He was proud of the final product, but his schoolmates teased him about the shirt.

His teacher decided to use the internet to combat the teasing. She posted the story on her Facebook page. The university saw her post and sent a box of memorabilia to the boy and his classmates. The university then decided to use the boy's T-shirt design and sell it, with some of the proceeds going to STOMP Out Bullying, an antibullying organization. The T-shirt was sold for three months and raised $952,101. The CEO of STOMP Out Bullying said, "We have always been an organization dedicated to spreading kindness and preventing bullying and cyberbullying, and this extremely generous donation helps us continue to make bullying history."

Quoted in "Shirt Designed by Fourth Grader Raises Nearly $1M for STOMP Out Bullying," The University of Tennessee Knoxville: News, *December 11, 2019. http://news.utk.edu.*

would stop. This is a misunderstanding of the nature of cyberbullying. Even if the teen is not online, the cyberbullying can continue. Nasty communications and photos can still be posted by the bully and shared with others online. The bullying may follow the teen to school through the devices of other students.

Not only is taking the victim offline ineffective in stopping cyberbullying, but the target is kept from the benefits of cyberspace when the bully is not. Randi Weingarten, the president of American Federation of Teachers (AFT), writes that interventions into bullying situations frequently involve the victim—rather than the bully—changing buses, classrooms, or even schools. She writes, "These are just a few of the 'solutions' that require the child who has behaved properly to change or move or adapt. This approach simply is not fair, and without a doubt, the children who have been bullied see and understand and *feel* the injustice of it."[13]

Bullying also continues because society views it as simply an unavoidable part of growing up—a "kids will be kids" mentality. Many people believe when bullying behavior occurs, the victim comes through it as a more mature and resilient person. However, experts are trying to change these incorrect ideas. Weingarten writes, "There is nothing natural about terrifying a child, or about one kid assaulting another simply for the sport of it, or about spreading vicious falsehoods about a teenager through the lunch line at school or across the digital channels of the Internet."[14] She further says that the safety of all children must be a priority and bullying should not be acceptable behavior.

> **"There is nothing natural about terrifying a child, or about one kid assaulting another simply for the sport of it, or about spreading vicious falsehoods about a teenager through the lunch line at school or across the digital channels of the Internet."[14]**
>
> ***—Randi Weingarten, president of the American Federation of Teachers***

CHAPTER TWO

HOW DOES CYBERBULLYING AFFECT TEENS?

Cyberbullying is often connected to bullying at school. Jennifer Obrizok, a school psychologist in Millbrook, New York, says that bullying at school can be continued through electronic means. For example, those students who are bullying might take a video of the target tripping and falling at school and post the embarrassing video online. Bullying can also move from cyberspace to the school setting. Screenshots of bullying comments made online may be passed around at school. Because cyberbullying and bullying in school are often linked, the target frequently feels unable to escape being bullied.

VICTIMIZATION AND PSYCHOLOGICAL PROBLEMS

Cyberbullying can go hand in hand with psychological problems. Many studies find a connection between victims of cyberbullying

Cyberbullying can increase the risk of or worsen the symptoms of depression. Many people who are bullied feel socially isolated from their peers.

and depression. For example, Manuel Gámez-Guadix and his colleagues studied 1,021 adolescents between thirteen and seventeen years of age in Spain. They wrote, "CB [cyberbullying] victimization leads to an increase in depressive symptoms and depressive symptoms, in turn, increase the probability of CB."[15] They hypothesized that cyberbullying leads to isolation and loneliness, which can cause feelings of sadness and rejection.

In addition, adolescents who are depressed may lack social skills, which can make them targets for cyberbullying. People with depression can feel hopeless or worthless. Individuals with depression might have disruptions in sleep, meaning they either sleep too much or have trouble sleeping. Some might eat too much or lose their appetites. Often, people with depression do not find pleasure in doing what they used to enjoy. They may display a lack of energy or motivation. They might speak or move slowly. Irritability can also be a symptom of depression. People with depression might think about killing themselves. This is known as suicidal ideation.

It is important to understand that the action of cyberbullying can result in the victim dying by suicide. The National Center for Injury Prevention and Control (NCIPC) notes that those who report involvement in bullying behaviors have higher levels of suicide-related

SIGNS OF CYBERBULLYING

There are outward signs people can watch for if they suspect their sibling or friend is being cyberbullied. If the person spends a lot of time on digital devices, this could be an indication. When she is online, she may seem noticeably anxious or upset. She may be reluctant to go to school. She might quickly close the webpage or device when people enter the room.

In the book *Cyberbullying and the Wild Wild Web: What Everyone Needs to Know*, J.A. Hitchcock outlines some warning signs that someone could be cyberbullying others. Again, the person might spend lots of time on digital devices and not let people see what he does online. He may have been involved in bullying at school, either as the aggressor or the victim.

behaviors. Often, the cases of cyberbullying that are covered by the media are those that end tragically in suicide. These are sad and shocking incidents that catch the attention of the media and the public. However, it is equally important to understand that cyberbullying usually does not end in suicide. The NCIPC wrote, "We know that most youth who are involved in bullying do NOT engage in suicide-related behavior."[16] The National Suicide Prevention Lifeline is a twenty-four-hour hotline available to people who are struggling with thoughts of suicide. The lifeline can be reached at 1-800-273-8255 (TALK) or online at suicidepreventionlifeline.org

Targets of cyberbullying can have anxiety. Individuals with anxiety have a general feeling of fearfulness or worry. They often feel restless or on edge. They might be irritable or tire quickly. Their sleep can be disturbed as well. Robin Kowalski and Susan Limber studied 931 students in grades six through twelve. They wrote, "Correlational analyses indicate that depression [and] anxiety . . . were significantly related to students' involvement in cyberbullying others, being cyberbullied, bullying others through traditional means, and being bullied through traditional means."[17]

People with anxiety might have panic attacks. Symptoms of a panic attack include a racing heart and shortness of breath. A person having a panic attack might shake and feel dizzy or feel out of control. During a panic attack, the person may experience depersonalization, which means that he feels disconnected from his own body or his own thinking. He might not recognize his voice as his own. He may also experience derealization. Derealization makes the person feel like his or her surroundings are not real. A person experiencing derealization often describes it as similar to being in a dream.

Cyberbullying victims might turn to alcohol and drug use as a way to deal with their psychological pain. Deborah Goebert and her colleagues studied 677 students from two high schools in Hawaii. They found a connection between serious mental health issues and cyberbullying, "with the greatest impact on substance use and suicide attempts." They wrote, "Experiencing cyberbullying tripled the likelihood of binge drinking and more than doubled the likelihood of using marijuana."[18] Substance use is an unhealthy way to cope, however. Substance use can compromise a person's physical health. It often negatively affects relationships with family and friends. Using substances can interfere with productivity at school and work. The person might also have trouble with the law if the substances are illegal or if he or she is underage.

Those being cyberbullied might also develop eating disorders. Jose H. Marco and M. Pilar Tormo-Irun studied 676 adolescents in Spain. They discovered that those who were cyberbullied felt dissatisfied with their bodies. They wrote,

Many victims of cyberbullying misuse drugs and alcohol. Cyberbullying and in-person bullying have long-term effects on psychological and physical health.

"Cyber victimization was associated with eating disorder psychopathy."[19] Eating disorders include anorexia nervosa, in which people believe they are overweight and severely limit their food intake, and bulimia nervosa, in which people eat large amounts and then purge by vomiting, using laxatives, or exercising excessively to compensate for food intake.

Dr. Christopher Sarampote of the National Institute of Mental Health (NIMH) said that targets of bullying can have psychosomatic issues, which are physical problems caused by psychological factors. The victims might suffer from headaches or stomachaches. Sarampote noted that there is literature "suggesting that immune system functioning is affected by peer victimization and trauma."[20] Lowered immunity affects the individual's ability to fight off physical illnesses, such as those caused by viruses. Sarampote also mentions that lowered immunity can negatively affect a person's cognitive and emotional health.

REHTAEH PARSONS

UnSlut: A Documentary Film recounts the story of Rehtaeh Parsons, who was a fifteen-year-old girl from Halifax, Nova Scotia, and the target of cyberbullying. In November 2011, she went to a friend's house for a sleepover. Her friend suggested that they visit two boys who lived nearby. Rehtaeh agreed to go. Soon, other boys came to the house. The group drank vodka. Rehtaeh was allegedly gang raped by the boys.

A boy was penetrating Rehtaeh from behind while she was naked from the waist down and vomiting out a window. Another boy took a photo of them. The photo was shared widely via text message. Before Rehtaeh had the chance to tell her side of what happened, the boys went to school and spread the story that Rehtaeh was a "slut."

A friend who had known Rehtaeh since she was five years old called her a slut on Facebook, which hurt her terribly. Rehtaeh became isolated. She was afraid to go to school and face the bullying. Her parents moved and enrolled her in a different high school to escape the cruelty. However, the story had already spread to the new school through the internet.

Rehtaeh sought the help of a therapist. She was diagnosed with depression. She turned to drug and alcohol use as an unhealthy way of coping with her experience. On April 4, 2013, Rehtaeh attempted suicide. When her mother discovered her, she had a slight pulse. Rehtaeh was declared brain dead on April 7. Rehtaeh's story was widely publicized, in spite of a ban that kept Canadian media outlets from reporting her name. In 2014, the boy who took the photo pleaded guilty to manufacturing child pornography. In early 2015, the boy in the photo was sentenced to a year of probation. Neither faced jail time. Rehtaeh's mother, Leah Parsons, said the cyberbullying was to blame for her daughter's death. "Rehtaeh is gone today because of the four boys that thought that raping a 15-year-old girl was OK and to distribute a photo to ruin her spirit and reputation would be fun. All the bullying and messaging and harassment that never let up are also to blame. Lastly, the justice system failed her. Those are the people that took the life of my beautiful girl."[21]

> "All the bullying and messaging and harassment that never let up are also to blame. . . . Those are the people that took the life of my beautiful girl."[21]
>
> *—Leah Parsons, on her daughter Rehtaeh's death by suicide*

SELF-ESTEEM, EMOTIONS, AND BEHAVIOR

In their 2012 study of cyberbullying, Sameer Hinduja and Justin W. Patchin found that cyberbullying victims, those engaged as cyberbullying aggressors, and those who were both victims and aggressors had lower self-esteem than those not involved in cyberbullying. This result regarding self-esteem is correlational, meaning that there is a connection between lower self-esteem and cyberbullying. However, the research does not prove that being a cyberbullying target or aggressor *causes* low self-esteem. The researchers note that the lower self-esteem might have been present before the cyberbullying. They wonder if those with lower self-esteem are simply more likely to be targets or bullies.

Those who are targets of cyberbullying report particular emotional effects. In their research, Hinduja and Patchin discovered that "many cyberbullying victims felt angry, frustrated, sad, embarrassed, or scared."[22] Hinduja and Patchin theorized that these emotional effects might be connected to behaviors such as violence and self-harm, but they determined that more investigation was needed.

There are certain behaviors seen with victims of traditional bullying. Because cyberbullying and in-school bullying often coincide, these behaviors can hold true for victims of

Victims of cyberbullying may skip school because they do not feel safe. This can lead to further social isolation and targeting by bullies.

cyberbullying as well. Sarampote says, "Kids who are bullied may avoid school. They may do poorly in school. They tend to be more truant and drop out more often."[23] Truancy, or skipping school, can be a problem for bullying targets. Because the victims are missing school, they may demonstrate a decrease in academic performance. Because they are afraid to go to school, they often become socially isolated as well.

Cyberbullying expert Parry Aftab describes behavior in which the target of bullying becomes the cyberbully. She categorizes

The effects of childhood bullying can linger in adulthood. Studies have shown that those who have been bullied have worse physical and mental health when they are older.

these cyberbullies as "vengeful angels." She writes, "In this type of cyberbullying, the cyberbully doesn't see themselves as the bully at all. They see themselves as righting wrongs or protecting themselves or others from the 'bad guy' they are now victimizing."[24] This type of person might have been bullied or cyberbullied and takes revenge by bullying the bully. This person views his or her actions as justifiable, but it is still bullying behavior. Perpetuating bullying is not the right way to handle victimization.

EFFECTS OF BULLYING INTO ADULTHOOD

Bullying should not be viewed as a harmless rite of passage or as a ritual of adolescence that everyone must go through. Dr. Robyn Silverman describes the long-term impact of bullying: “Bullying doesn’t just have legs—it has teeth. The memories hold on tightly even as we leave our school days behind.”[25] It is not only the negative memories that remain. The psychological effects of bullying also continue into adulthood.

> **“Bullying doesn’t just have legs—it has teeth. The memories hold on tightly even as we leave our school days behind.”[25]**
>
> ***—Robyn Silverman, child and adolescent development specialist***

Dr. William Copeland of Duke University and his colleagues studied whether the effects of teen bullying continued into adulthood. They conducted a study in which they followed children ages nine to sixteen for two decades. They categorized the children as victims only, bully and victim (bully/victim), bully only, and neither. Their research concluded that victims had higher rates of anxiety disorders in adulthood. Copeland notes, though, that in adulthood, the bully/victims fared the worst psychologically. He says the bully/victims “had about five times higher risk of depression and five times higher risk of suicidal thoughts and behavior, as well as risks for some anxiety disorders too."[26] Bullying, therefore, does not make the victims more resilient as was once believed. Instead, it can result in lasting psychological damage.

> "[Bully/victims] had about five times higher risk of depression and five times higher risk of suicidal thoughts and behavior, as well as risks for some anxiety disorders too."[26]
>
> *—William Copeland, professor of psychiatry*

AMANDA TODD

Amanda Todd of Port Coquitlam, British Columbia, was in the seventh grade and used a webcam to speak with other people on BlogTV, a livestreaming website. One time, she was encouraged to flash her breasts for the camera. When she did, a person took a screenshot.

A year later, Amanda received a message on Facebook from a stranger. He said that if she didn't put on a show for him, he would release the photo of her breasts on the internet. The person knew her address, school, and names of her friends and family members. Amanda refused, and he released the photo.

Amanda experienced cyberbullying and in-school bullying by fellow students who called her names such as "cam whore" and "porn star."[27] Amanda had panic attacks and depression. She was afraid to go out. She was isolated and lonely, and she turned to drugs and alcohol to cope.

Cyberstalking occurs when the aggressor follows the target using many different digital methods in order to cyberbully. Amanda changed schools, but the cyberstalker created a Facebook page with her breast photo as his profile picture. When the students at the new school saw this, the bullying began again. Again, she switched schools. Things were going better. She met a boy and began a relationship with him. But he had a girlfriend, and she beat Amanda in front of fifty other students. Afterwards, Amanda tried to take her own life. When she came home from the hospital, there were cruel comments posted online about her suicide attempt. People wrote, "She deserved it," and "I hope she's dead."[28]

In September 2012, Amanda created a video in which she used written cards to silently describe the impact that cyberbullying and traditional bullying had on her life. She posted the video on YouTube. Millions of people have watched it.

On October 10, 2012, Amanda died by suicide. Her cyberstalker was finally caught by the police after her death. He was a man in his midthirties from the Netherlands. He was found guilty in similar cyberbullying cases and sentenced to almost eleven years in prison in the Netherlands. In early 2020, he was awaiting extradition to Canada to be tried in Amanda's case.

Cyberbullying can lead to legal consequences. Many cyberbullying crimes are classified as harassment.

THOSE WHO BULLY

Joel Haber says that those who bully lack empathy. They do not consider the pain their targets experience. In addition, bullies often have self-control issues and may have violence in their homes or communities. According to StopBullying.gov, a website managed by the US Department of Health and Human Services, those who engage in bullying behavior tend to use alcohol and drugs to excess both as teens and as adults. In adulthood, former bullies are more likely to be abusive toward their significant others, spouses, and children.

Copeland and his fellow researchers found that "Bullies were at increased risk for antisocial personality disorder."[29] Individuals with antisocial personality disorder demonstrate social irresponsibility that can result in criminal behavior. Copeland also found that bullies are more likely to be aggressive at home and work.

Journalist and Yale Lecturer in Law Emily Bazelon writes that bullies often end up with criminal convictions later in life. Bullies are four times more likely than others to become criminals. She references a study by the respected Olweus Bullying Prevention Program, an antibullying program for schools, which concludes that "60 percent of childhood bullies end up with at least one conviction; between 35 and 40 percent have three or more."[30]

CONSIDER THE INDIVIDUAL

It is important to consider the participants in cyberbullying and bullying as individuals. Jennifer Obrizok doesn't like to label those involved in bullying of any sort as *victim* or *bully*. She says, "People are multifaceted." To label people is to run the risk that they will identify themselves with those terms.

Health educator Meghan Miller works to empower targets of bullying so they do not view themselves as victims. She focuses on improving the target's self-esteem and teaching assertiveness. In addition, Miller wants others to understand the problems underlying bullying behavior. Those who bully often come from home or community environments where they are targets of bullying or violence, or witnesses to bullying behavior or violence. When they engage in bullying, it is frequently an attempt to gain control that they don't have in their home or community environment. Many times, those who bully don't know how to cope with their emotions in healthy ways. They likely have self-control or anger issues that can be addressed in counseling. It is important to not lose sight of the person behind the behavior.

Jennifer Obrizok, Personal interview, November 24, 2019.

CHAPTER THREE

HOW DOES TEEN CYBERBULLYING AFFECT SOCIETY?

Members of particular societal groups are often targets of cyberbullying and traditional bullying. Some of these targeted societal groups include lesbian, gay, bisexual, transgender, and queer/questioning (LGBTQ) individuals, women, those with special needs, people experiencing homelessness, and children of military service members.

WOMEN AS CYBERBULLYING TARGETS

Research shows that girls are more likely to be targets of cyberbullying than boys. Some of the cyberbullying girls and women face takes the form of slut-shaming. Slut-shaming is the way that society negatively portrays a woman's sexual behavior. Women are marked with the reputation of "slut" or "whore"

Monica Lewinsky faced cyberbullying and slut-shaming after her relationship with President Clinton became public. She has since become an advocate against cyberbullying.

when they act on their sexual desires. Men are rarely judged in this manner, which demonstrates a double standard. In fact, the same type of sexual activity in men is often encouraged and praised by society.

Monica Lewinsky was twenty-four years old in 1998 when her sexual relationship with her boss, US President Bill Clinton, was made public. In her 2015 TED talk, Lewinsky discussed the impact of that time in her life. She went from being a private citizen to the target of worldwide cyberbullying overnight. Although there was no social media then, the news stories were reported online. The public posted cruel messages in the comment sections following the articles, and they sent her upsetting emails. They called her "tramp" and "whore." This public shaming was nearly unbearable for Lewinsky. In her TED talk, she said, "In 1998, I lost my reputation and my dignity. I lost almost everything. And I almost lost my life."[31]

Lewinsky credits the compassion she received from family, friends, and even strangers for pulling her through this depressed period. In her talk, she makes a plea for acting with compassion online. She says, "What we need is a cultural revolution. Public shaming as a blood sport has to stop. And it's time for an intervention on the internet, and in our culture. The shift begins with something simple, but it's not easy. We need to return to a long-held value of compassion—compassion and empathy. Online we've got a compassion deficit, an empathy crisis."[32] She notes that clicking on stories that feed on the humiliation of others is just a way to put money into the pockets of the websites running those stories. She advised clicking with compassion.

> **"What we need is a cultural revolution. Public shaming as a blood sport has to stop. And it's time for an intervention on the internet, and in our culture. . . . Online we've got a compassion deficit, an empathy crisis."[32]**
>
> ***—Monica Lewinsky, antibullying activist***

Like Lizzie Velásquez, Lewinsky has taken her experience as a cyberbullying target and channeled those feelings to become an activist. She is driven to put an end to cyberbullying. And she offers these words of hope for targets of cyberbullying: "You can survive it. . . . You can insist on a different end for your story."[33]

In a romantic relationship, people may send a sexually revealing photo of themselves to their significant other. If the relationship ends badly, the other person might angrily share the photo with others via social media or text. This victimization is commonly called *revenge porn* and is another type of cyberbullying that men and women endure, though women experience it more often. Yanet Ruvalcaba and Asia A. Eaton surveyed 3,044 people and found, "Women experienced higher rates of nonconsensual pornography victimization than men."[34] The purpose of revenge porn is to publicly humiliate a person for his or her sexual behavior.

> "Women experienced higher rates of nonconsensual pornography victimization than men."[34]
>
> —*Yanet Ruvalcaba and Asia A. Eaton*

CYBERBULLYING OF LGBTQ INDIVIDUALS

The statistics demonstrate that those who are LGBTQ are cyberbullied more often than those who are not. In 2010, Tyler Clementi was a freshman at Rutgers University in New Jersey.

Those who identify as part of the LGBTQ community are likely to experience cyberbullying. Support systems and allies are important for victims of bullying.

Clementi was a gay man who had just begun to come out to his close family and friends. He was a talented violinist, one of only two freshman students chosen to play in Rutgers University's graduate school orchestra.

One night, Clementi asked his roommate, Dharun Ravi, to give him privacy for a date. Ravi secretly turned on his webcam and streamed the video. The video recorded Clementi and his male date being intimate. Ravi then wrote about the incident on Twitter and attempted to stream a video again a few days later. Clementi was the topic of humiliating commentary.

Eighteen-year-old Clementi died by suicide several days later. The cyberbullying he underwent may have contributed to his suicide.

In 2012, Ravi was convicted of fifteen counts, including privacy invasion and bias intimidation. Bias intimidation is charged when a person's criminal actions are motivated by the victim's race, religion, or sexual orientation. However, the New Jersey Supreme Court eventually ruled the bias intimidation laws were unconstitutional, and Ravi's convictions were overturned. In the end, he pleaded guilty to attempted privacy invasion.

CYBERBULLYING OF THOSE WITH SPECIAL NEEDS

Students with special needs are often the targets of cyberbullying and bullying. James H. Wendorf, former executive director for the National Center for Learning Disabilities, says, "For students with learning disabilities and other disabilities, bullying is a pandemic. It occurs every day, with 60 percent of students with special needs being bullied as compared to 25 percent of all students—and there are some studies that put this percentage even higher."[35]

"For students with learning disabilities and other disabilities, bullying is a pandemic."[35]

—James H. Wendorf, former executive director for the National Center for Learning Disabilities

Students with learning disabilities are often targets for bullying. Peer support is important in fostering relationships and teaching students empathy.

Donna Desimone is the program director at Community Steps to Independence, a program for eighteen- to twenty-one-year-old individuals with special needs who have completed their high school requirements and are learning to live independently. She says, "Every single one of my students was bullied when they were younger."[36] Desimone says that the students without special needs viewed Desimone's students as different and targeted them. She says perhaps they were perceived as different because many of her students lack social skills and some have difficulty communicating. To help their students fit in better, Desimone and her colleagues spend a lot of time teaching social skills. For example, they practice how to have conversations with others.

Even though Desimone and fellow educators teach the students about cybersafety, the students often disregard the warnings. "They so badly want friends," she says, and they seek those friendships online.[37] Her students have been victims of cyberbullying and catfishing, which happens when a person pretends to be someone else online.

Desimone talks about an effective program that the Cresskill Middle School Student Organization runs. Two students from each grade are chosen to interact with Desimone's class. Her students plan and hold three events each year for the younger ones. Through these events, the younger children gain an appreciation for students with special needs. "The whole point is to build more understanding, to build empathy," says Desimone.[38] Those with empathy are less likely to bully. Desimone has seen the heartwarming successes of the

> "The whole point is to build more understanding, to build empathy."[38]
>
> *—Donna Desimone, Program Instructor of Community Steps to Independence*

middle school program. Now, the younger students wave and say hello whenever they pass her students. When one group of middle schoolers who had participated in the program became seniors in high school, they reached out and invited Desimone's class to join in their Senior Year Day. They all went bowling and out to dinner together.

CYBERBULLYING AND HOMELESSNESS

Meghan Miller, MPH, is the director of health education at the Floating Hospital in Long Island City, Queens, New York. The Floating Hospital is a charity hospital that serves people who live in homeless shelters and domestic violence shelters. Many of the young people with whom Miller works are targets of cyberbullying and traditional bullying.

According to the New York City Youth Risk Behavior Survey of 2015, 18.5 percent of students who lost their homes or could not afford housing were cyberbullied as compared to 12 percent of students who had not lost their homes. The same survey showed that 18.4 percent of students who lost their homes or could not afford housing were bullied in school as compared to 14 percent of students who had not lost their homes. Miller says that bullies target students without homes for a variety of reasons. For one, they often have to change schools when they lose their homes. Being new at school and initially without friends

Students struggling with financial difficulties are about twice as likely to be victims of bullying as those from wealthier families. Family income is a strong predictor for whether someone will experience bullying.

can make them targets. In addition, homelessness often goes hand in hand with low economic status. These students don't have the money to purchase clothes that are in fashion. This lack of money can mean that they have a limited wardrobe and wear the same clothes frequently. Because the clothes are worn often, they might not be clean. Also, the students don't always have the money for laundromat services or laundry detergent. These students might not have the means to buy toiletries, such as deodorant or shampoo, to maintain hygiene. Bullies who don't understand the challenges these students face might target them for any of these reasons.

CYBERBULLYING LAWS

As of 2020, there are no federal laws in the United States that address cyberbullying or bullying specifically. However, civil rights laws cover discriminatory harassment when it applies to a person's race, national origin, color, sex, age, disability, or religion. These laws might apply to certain cyberbullying or bullying situations.

There are states, however, that have antibullying laws, policies, or regulations. According to StopBullying.gov, most states "require districts and schools to implement a bullying policy and procedures to investigate and respond to bullying when it occurs. A handful

CYBERBULLYING AND MILITARY KIDS

The children of military service members are vulnerable to bullying and cyberbullying. According to the website StopBullying.gov, the average military child will undergo nine changes of school between kindergarten and senior year in high school. These frequent transitions mean periods with few or no friends and possible academic struggles, which can make them targets for bullies.

If a military parent is deployed, the student can have added responsibilities at home and worries about the safety of the deployed parent, which can result in the student feeling anxious and depressed. Anxiety and depression can make them more likely to be bullied.

of states also require bullying prevention programs, inclusion of bullying prevention in health education standards, and/or teacher professional development."[39]

> "[Most states] require districts and schools to implement a bullying policy and procedures to investigate and respond to bullying when it occurs."[39]
>
> —*StopBullying.gov*

The question of when schools can step in and address cyberbullying or discipline perpetrators is a tricky one. Students have a right to freedom of speech and freedom of expression, which schools cannot challenge. However, court cases have clarified that schools can address cyberbullying that causes substantial disruption in the educational environment or infringes upon the rights of others.

CHAPTER FOUR

HOW DO WE PREVENT TEEN CYBERBULLYING?

Many practical ways exist to prevent cyberbullying. Following safe online practices and teaching all students about empathy and dignity are some preventative measures. However, if cyberbullying occurs, there are also certain steps to take to address it effectively.

PROTECT PASSWORDS AND PERSONAL INFORMATION

The first line of defense against cyberbullying is to adopt safe online practices. People should choose complex, lengthy passwords for their digital accounts. They should not use something easy to decipher, such as their birthday. It is good to use a combination of uppercase and lowercase letters, numbers, and symbols. Additionally, different passwords should be used for each account. This way, if someone gains access

Two-factor authentication and strong passwords help protect accounts and private information. Using smart online practices prevents cyberbullies from being able to access personal information.

to one account, the rest will not be compromised. People can use password managers to manage and generate complex passwords and not have to remember them all. A person should not share passwords with others who might not be careful with the passwords.

Many experts recommend using a two-factor authentication system for an added layer of security. With this system, when someone logs into a website, a code is sent to another digital device that the person has chosen, such as a phone. This code needs to be entered to gain access. There is little chance that someone who uncovers the password would also have the second device handy to retrieve the authentication code.

Jennifer Obrizok says people should be careful about what they post online. They shouldn't post comments that include personal information. For example, a person's home address, telephone number, school name, or grade level shouldn't be mentioned. People should not "check in" with their location at their home address. Shared photos can unintentionally reveal personal information as well. A person might be wearing a sweatshirt with her school name on it. In addition, technology allows people to zoom in on photos and see small identifying items. Perhaps the mailbox in the background of a photo has the individual's address on it.

Obrizok advises caution when communicating with strangers. Though someone could claim to be a peer, this might not be the case. Obrizok warns that it could be a middle-aged man posing as a young person. Megan Meier and Amanda Todd both encountered this type of catfishing situation.

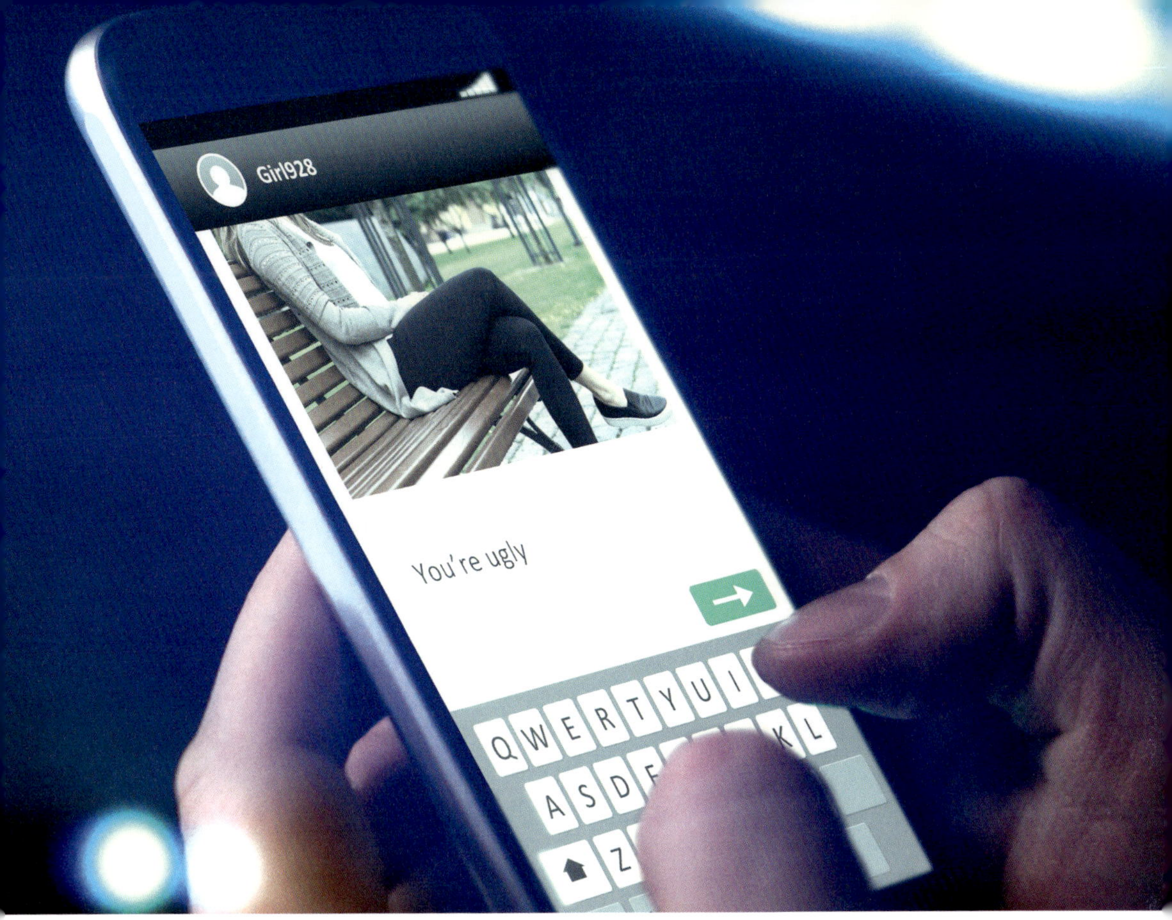

Victims should screenshot and save cyberbullying comments to be used as evidence. They should avoid responding to hurtful comments in a way that escalates tensions.

PROTECT REPUTATION AND PRIVACY

People have to be careful not to post comments or share photos that could compromise their reputations. Obrizok warns about the "permanency of the Internet."[40] Things that are posted online are there indefinitely. Whatever is posted online today will be searchable long into the future, and it could interfere with acceptance to a top choice college or dream job.

There is a misunderstanding that risky posts can be easily deleted. This is not the case. Someone might take a screenshot of the post or share it before it is deleted. According to Sameer Hinduja and Justin W. Patchin, there are search engines and websites that archive web pages. For example, the Library of Congress archived every tweet from 2010 until 2017. From 2017 on, only some tweets will be archived.

Teens might be tempted to send one another nude photos. It is important to understand that if the people in the photos are under the age of eighteen, the images are considered child pornography, which is illegal. Whoever has the photos on their digital devices can be considered to be in possession of child pornography and can face charges. Another good reason for not sharing nude photos is that relationships can end tumultuously. Someone hurt by a breakup might decide to share the nude photo on social media or through text as an act of revenge porn.

Each social media site has a way to adjust privacy settings. People should make sure privacy settings only allow their photos and comments to be visible to people they choose. For example, Facebook allows a person to choose the audience for posts. The privacy setting might be set so only friends or friends of friends can see them. There is also a public setting that lets everyone see the individual's posts.

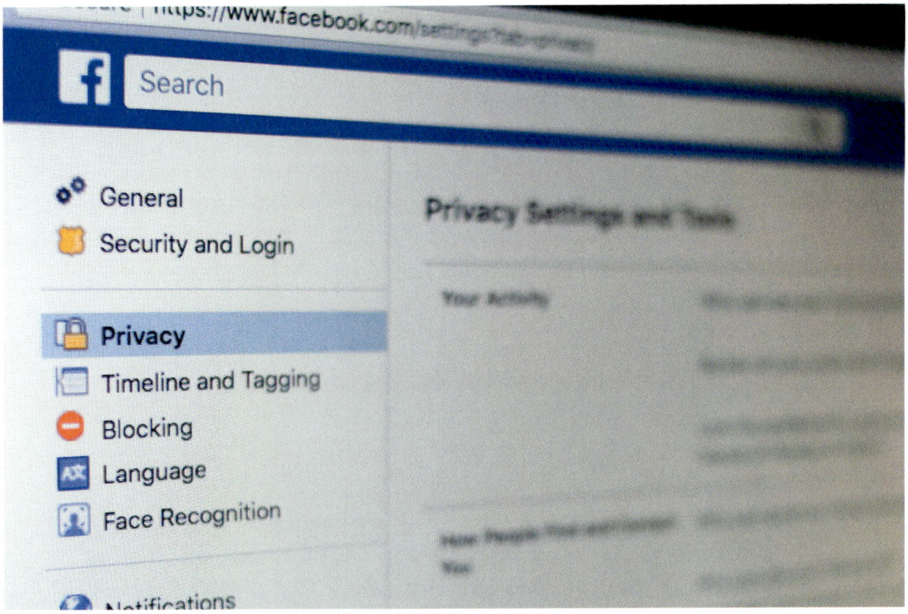

Increased privacy settings make information less public. Victims can also block or report bullies on social media to protect themselves.

Hinduja and Patchin recommend turning off location sharing features on digital media. It's not a good idea for a person to let others know where she is in real time. Acquaintances and even strangers could know her location. In addition, photos, videos, and text messages can have geotagging, which attaches certain data to them. The data can include the user's location. It is best to disable geotagging because it can also make the user vulnerable to unwanted attention.

LIMIT TIME ONLINE

The more time a person spends online, the more likely he or she is to be touched by cyberbullying. People should consider limiting the amount of time they spend on digital devices. Meghan Miller says that being online can keep people from spending time with friends in real life. It can keep them from having experiences out in the world, such as exploring hobbies and reading books. It can isolate them. Additionally, Obrizok warns that the light from digital devices' screens can interfere with sleep. Disrupted sleep can affect physical health and moods.

It is important to understand that social media is designed to manipulate. Receiving likes stimulates the reward center of the brain and makes a person feel good. On the other hand, not getting likes can leave a person feeling unhappy. The first president of Facebook, Sean Parker, spoke about this manipulation: "It's a social-validation feedback loop. It's exploiting a vulnerability in human psychology."[41]

> **"It's a social-validation feedback loop. It's exploiting a vulnerability in human psychology."[41]**
>
> ***—Sean Parker, former president of Facebook***

Also, people rarely post the negatives about their lives on social media. They don't often post about failing grades or fights with siblings. Instead, people post about fun times with friends or fabulous vacations. Miller says that an individual comparing herself with these unrealistic portrayals of others' lives can negatively affect the way she feels about herself.

Limiting screen time reduces the likelihood of being affected by cyberbullying. Reducing phone use can also improve quality of sleep.

STEPS TO TAKE IF CYBERBULLYING OCCURS

If a person is being cyberbullied, there are steps to take to try to put a stop to it. The individual needs to document the instances of cyberbullying. He should screenshot what is occurring. Journalist Misha Valencia writes, "Include the website or app name in the image and a picture of the commenter's profile."[42] The person should also print hard copies. To be considered cyberbullying, victimization must be repeated. The victim should keep a written record of what happened and when, and the victim should tell a trusted adult, such as a parent, teacher, or school counselor.

The victim needs to cut contact with the cyberbully. He can block the person from his social media account or block the person's number from his cell phone. Social media sites have terms of service that prohibit cyberbullying. The victim can report the cyberbullying to them directly. Valencia says to be certain to mention that a minor is the target. These companies can suspend the aggressor's account for cyberbullying.

If the cyberbullying is originating with fellow students at the target's school, the administration can be contacted. When the cyberbullying interferes with the educational environment, the school administrators can step in. In certain circumstances, the police should be contacted about cyberbullying. If there has been property damage, such as vandalism, the police can become involved. If a cyberstalker follows the target via email, social media, and texting, or if the cyberstalking morphs into stalking in real life, the victim should call the police. When there is blackmail or a threat of physical violence, the police need to be informed.

A lawyer may prove helpful in some situations. She might send a strongly worded letter to inform the cyberbully of the

Students should inform a trusted adult if they experience cyberbullying. These conversations are not always easy, but it is important to seek help to stay safe.

possible legal ramifications of the behavior. This might convince the bully to stop.

EMPOWERING THE CYBERBULLYING TARGET

Most experts advise targets of cyberbullying not to respond. Bullies are seeking to provoke the target. Ignore the behavior and the bully might give up. Obrizok warns that if the target reacts emotionally, it serves as a form of entertainment to the person bullying.

On the other hand, both Obrizok and Miller agree that targets of in-school bullying may choose to respond with confidence. This can dissuade bullying behavior. Miller teaches students to stay neutral emotionally and "deliver a one-liner like, 'Don't talk to me like that' or, 'O.K. Are you done?'" Miller advises to be "persistent with confident reactions" because it won't necessarily stop the bullying the first time.[43] Obrizok says it is important "to empower people to stick up for themselves; it is not healthy to be in a victim role."[44]

In the past, schools often placed the bullying target and bully in the same room to work out their differences. Educational psychologist Dr. Michele Borba writes, "Bullying is *not* a conflict, but an aggressive act."[45] These are not two peers having a disagreement. Instead, it is a case of one person victimizing another. Obrizok says that in her school, the target and the person who bullies are not placed together. However, in rare instances, the target might wish to confront the aggressor. In that case, everyone, including the parents of both students, must agree to a meeting. If everyone is in agreement, a specially trained mediator is brought in to help the target, aggressor, and both sets of parents communicate.

> **"Bullying is *not* a conflict, but an aggressive act."[45]**
>
> ***—Educational psychologist Dr. Michele Borba***

Extensive counseling precedes the mediation and continues afterward. This can be empowering for the target.

In the past, targets of cyberbullying and traditional bullying were forced to change their lives to avoid the bullying. Perhaps they had to stop using digital media or, in the instance of in-school bullying, had to switch classrooms or schools. Today, the person who bullies is more often given the consequences and is more likely to face these changes.

FRIENDSHIPS AND HIGHER SELF-ESTEEM CAN HELP

There are ways to help individuals better endure cyberbullying or bullying experiences. They may even be able to avoid them entirely. Bullying victims often do not have many friends. Therefore, a way to prevent or deal with bullying is to increase a person's number of friends. Obrizok says a good way to make friends is for a person to consider her interests and find people who share those interests. She could join extracurricular activities, such as a pottery club or the field hockey team. With more friends, a person is less likely to be targeted. But if he is targeted, he has a support system.

On the other hand, it might be necessary to move away from the school environment to find friends. Dr. Robyn Silverman calls this "diversifying" friendship circles. A person could take

Community clubs create an opportunity to make friends outside of school. Having new skills and hobbies can create a sense of identity and confidence for victims of cyberbullying.

lessons at a community dance studio or join a group that reads and discusses graphic novels. She writes, "If [a] teen is feeling particularly marginalized or cast out, finding a group that serves other teens like him or her can be a great comfort and resource."[46] Not only are these activities a solid method for making friends, they often provide the opportunity to master a skill. Silverman says that having an expertise "allows you to define yourself by your strengths rather than give permission to others to define you by any perceived deficits."[47] This sense of mastery breeds self-confidence and improves self-esteem, and improved self-esteem can help a person avoid or deal with bullying.

Volunteering provides a way to make friends with similar charitable leanings. Volunteers can also learn skills. Overall, reaching out to people who are in need can improve the way an individual views himself. Dr. Christine Carter writes, "Teens who volunteer tend to be more socially competent and have higher self-esteem."[48]

> "Teens who volunteer tend to be more socially competent and have higher self-esteem."[48]
>
> *—Dr. Christine Carter, Senior Fellow at UC Berkeley's Greater Good Science Center*

WHAT SCHOOLS ARE DOING

Experts find that bullies often lack empathy. Many schools are incorporating teachings that are designed to improve empathy and, in turn, prevent cases of cyberbullying and bullying. Schools are introducing lessons that focus on social-emotional learning (SEL) so that students treat one another with understanding and kindness. These lessons include learning to identify your feelings and the feelings of others and how to cope with different emotions. Students are taught about empathy. They learn about acting with compassion toward others and making responsible choices.

Postdoctoral researcher Tijana Milosevic and her colleagues discuss the importance of introducing dignity training to prevent cyberbullying. They point to Donna Hicks's work concerning dignity. Hicks defines dignity as a person's "inherent value and worth" and says that each person is "equally worthy of having that dignity honored."[49] Hicks's elements of dignity include acceptance of identity, or the idea that no one person is better or worse than another; inclusion of others; and acknowledgment, or giving people your full attention. Learning to honor one another's dignity will reduce the incidences of cyberbullying and bullying.

TRISHA PRABHU: HIGH-TECH UPSTANDER

In 2013, thirteen-year-old Trisha Prabhu was saddened and angry when she read that twelve-year-old Rebecca Sedwick died by suicide after years of being cyberbullied. She was determined to help stop cyberbullying.

Prabhu designed the ReThink app for iPhone and Android. It is a digital keyboard that uses artificial intelligence to determine if what is being typed is objectionable. If so, it gives the user a pop-up alert, giving the user time to reconsider sending the text message or posting on social media. The technology is proving effective. The company cites research demonstrating that when using ReThink, the willingness of adolescents to post an objectionable comment was reduced from 71 percent to 4 percent.

As of 2020, Prabhu is a student at Harvard University. Her next goal is to design a way to detect objectionable images and allow users to pause and decide not to send or post them.

Some schools create a particular program focused on improving the school environment to prevent or curb bullying behavior. Patchin and Hinduja highlight Lake Brantley High School in Altamonte Springs, Florida, for instituting its

Those who witness cyberbullying or bullying can stand up for victims. They might provide support to the victim or inform an adult of the situation.

"To Be Kind" program. This program encourages kind and positive actions between students. Other times, schools turn to outside sources for antibullying programs, such as the Olweus Bullying Prevention Program, to prevent and reduce instances of bullying and improve student relationships.

HOW CAN OTHER TEENS LEND SUPPORT?

Miller advises her students not to join in the cyberbullying behavior. She tells them if rumors or gossip come across digital

It is important for people to support and care about others. Fostering kindness and empathy can help put a stop to cyberbullying.

media, do not share them. When someone is making mean comments on social media, do not add to them.

Miller suggests that bystanders, those who observe cyberbullying or bullying, don't have to just watch. Instead, they can help the victim. If a person sees that hurtful things are being written to someone online, Miller suggests that an upstander—one who stands up against bullying—might create a positive post to include on the target's social media page. A kind comment can offset a cruel one.

Miller says that if the bully is of similar power or social status as the upstander, the upstander can confront the bully directly. After a bullying incident, the upstander might say, "That was not cool." However, an upstander does not have to confront the bully directly; she can provide support to the victim in other ways. She might be able to remove the victim from the bullying situation. She can encourage the victim to tell an adult or can report the incident herself. Miller suggests that following a bullying instance, the upstander can offer supportive words. Obrizok says an upstander might offer to walk the target to class. "There really is safety in numbers," according to Obrizok.[50]

Cyberbullying can have devastating effects on those involved. But there are concrete ways to avoid or deal with cyberbullying. If people approach online behavior with empathy and kindness, everyone can lead happier and more peaceful lives. Standing up to perpetrators can help show targets that others care; they are not alone.

SOURCE NOTES

INTRODUCTION: TRIUMPH OVER CYBERBULLYING

1. Quoted in *A Brave Heart: The Lizzie Velasquez Story*. Directed by Sara Hirsh Bordo, The Lizzie Project, 2015.
2. Quoted in *A Brave Heart*.
3. Quoted in *A Brave Heart*.
4. Quoted in *A Brave Heart*.
5. Quoted in *A Brave Heart*.
6. Quoted in *A Brave Heart*.

CHAPTER 1: WHAT IS TEEN CYBERBULLYING?

7. Quoted in Steve Pokin, "Megan's Story," *Megan Meier Foundation*, November 13, 2007. https://meganmeierfoundation.org.
8. Quoted in "Megan Meier Foundation," *Megan Meier Foundation*, n.d. https://meganmeierfoundation.org.
9. Nancy E. Willard, *Cyberbullying and Cyberthreats: Responding to the Challenge of Online Social Aggression, Threats, and Distress*. Champaign, IL: Research Press, 2007, p. 10.
10. Lee Hirsch and Cynthia Lowen with Dina Santorelli, eds, *Bully: An Action Plan for Teachers, Parents, and Communities to Combat the Bullying Crisis*. New York: Weinstein Books, 2012, p. 6.
11. Joel Haber, "What Types of Children Bully?" *KidsInTheHouse*, 2019. www.kidsinthehouse.com.
12. Sameer Hinduja and Justin W. Patchin, *Bullying Beyond the Schoolyard: Preventing and Responding to Cyberbullying*. Thousand Oaks, CA: Corwin, 2015, p. 64.
13. Quoted in Hirsch, *Bully*, p. 118.
14. Quoted in Hirsch, *Bully*, p. 117.

CHAPTER 2: HOW DOES CYBERBULLYING AFFECT TEENS?

15. Manuel Gámez-Guadix, Izaskun Orue, et al., "Longitudinal and Reciprocal Relations of Cyberbullying with Depression, Substance Use, and Problematic Internet Use Among Adolescents." *Journal of Adolescent Health*. Vol. 52, Issue 4, October 2013, pp. 446–452.
16. Quoted in "The Relationship Between Bullying and Suicide: What We Know and What It Means for Schools," *CDC*, n.d. www.cdc.gov.
17. Robin Kowalski and Susan Limber, "Psychological, Physical, and Academic Correlation of Cyberbullying and Traditional Bullying." *Journal of Adolescent Health*. Vol. 53, Issue 1, July 2013, pp. S13–S20.
18. Deborah Goebert, Iwalani Else, Courtenay Matsu, Jane Chung-Do, and Janice Y. Chang, "The Impact of Cyberbullying on Substance Use and Mental Health in a Multiethnic Sample." *Maternal and Child Health Journal*. Vol. 15, September 8, 2010, pp. 1282–1286.

19. Jose H. Marco and M. Pilar Tormo-Irun, "Cyber Victimization Is Associated with Eating Disorder Psychopathology in Adolescents," *Frontiers in Psychology*, June 14, 2018, p. 987.

20. William Copeland and Christopher Sarampote, "Bullying Exerts Psychiatric Effects into Adulthood," *NIMH*, April 11, 2013. www.nimh.nih.gov.

21. Quoted in Paula Newton, "Canadian Teen Commits Suicide After Alleged Rape, Bullying," *CNN*, April 10, 2013. www.cnn.com.

22. Hinduja and Patchin, *Bullying Beyond the Schoolyard*, p. 92.

23. Copeland and Sarampote, "Bullying Exerts Psychiatric Effects into Adulthood."

24. Parry Aftab, "What Methods Work with Different Kinds of Cyberbullies," *WiredSafety*, n.d. www.stopcyberbullying.org.

25. Hirsch, *Bully*, p. 48.

26. Copeland and Sarampote, "Bullying Exerts Psychiatric Effects into Adulthood."

27. Quoted in "The Sextortion of Amanda Todd—The Fifth Estate," *YouTube*, uploaded by CBC/Radio-Canada, August 11, 2014. www.youtube.com.

28. "My Story: Struggling, Bullying, Suicide, Self-Harm," *YouTube*, uploaded by Amanda Todd, September 7, 2012. www.youtube.com.

29. William Copeland, Dieter Wolke, Adrian Angold, and E. Jane Costello, "Adult Psychiatric and Suicide Outcomes of Bullying and Being Bullied by Peers in Adolescence." *JAMA Psychiatry*. Vol. 70, Issue 4, April 2013, pp. 419–426.

30. Emily Bazelon, *Sticks and Stones: Defeating the Culture of Bullying and Rediscovering the Power of Character and Empathy*. New York: Random House, 2013, p. 31.

CHAPTER 3: HOW DOES TEEN CYBERBULLYING AFFECT SOCIETY?

31. Monica Lewinsky, "The Price of Shame," *TED*, March 20, 2015. www.ted.com.

32. Lewinsky, "The Price of Shame."

33. Lewinsky, "The Price of Shame."

34. Yanet Ruvalcaba and Asia A. Eaton, "Nonconsensual Pornography Among US Adults: A Sexual Scripts Framework on Victimization, Perpetration, and Health Correlates for Women and Men," *Psychology of Violence*, 2019. www.cybercivilrights.org.

35. Hirsch, *Bully*, p. 106.

36. Donna Desimone, Personal interview, January 5, 2020.

37. Donna Desimone, Personal interview, January 5, 2020.

38. Donna Desimone, Personal interview, January 5, 2020.

SOURCE NOTES CONTINUED

39. "Laws, Policies & Regulations," *StopBullying.gov*, n.d. www.stopbullying.gov.

CHAPTER 4: HOW DO WE PREVENT TEEN CYBERBULLYING?

40. Jennifer Obrizok, Personal interview, November 24, 2019.

41. Quoted in Will Geddes with Nadia Sawalha and Kaye Adams, *Parent Alert! How to Keep Your Kids Safe Online*. New York: DK, 2018, p. 50.

42. Misha Valencia, "How to Safeguard Children Against Cyberbullying," *New York Times*, September 5, 2019. www.nytimes.com.

43. Meghan Miller, Personal interview, January 2, 2020.

44. Jennifer Obrizok, Personal interview, November 24, 2019.

45. Hirsch, *Bully*, p. 187.

46. Hirsch, *Bully*, p. 53.

47. Hirsch, *Bully*, p. 58.

48. Christine Carter, "What We Get When We Give," *Psychology Today*, February 19, 2010. www.psychologytoday.com.

49. Donna Hicks, "Declare Dignity," *Dr. Donna Hicks*, n.d. https://drdonnahicks.com.

50. Jennifer Obrizok, Personal interview, November 24, 2019.

FOR FURTHER RESEARCH

BOOKS

Melissa Abramovitz, *Online Predators*. San Diego, CA: ReferencePoint Press, 2017.

Tammy Gagne, *Online Shaming and Bullying*. San Diego, CA: ReferencePoint Press, 2020.

Jeff Mapua, *Coping with Cyberbullying*. New York: Rosen Publishing, 2018.

Hal Marcovitz, *Thinking Critically: Cyberbullying*. San Diego, CA: ReferencePoint Press, 2015.

Derek Miller, *Dealing with Cyberbullying*. New York: Cavendish Square, 2020.

INTERNET SOURCES

"Information and Answers to Frequently Asked Questions About Cyberbullying," *National Crime Prevention Council*, n.d. www.ncpc.org.

US Department of Health and Human Services, "Bystanders to Bullying," *StopBullying.gov*, n.d. www.stopbullying.gov.

Misha Valencia, "How to Safeguard Children Against Cyberbullying," *New York Times*, September 5, 2019. www.nytimes.com.

WEBSITES

AMAZE
https://amaze.org

This website addresses all sorts of timely teen concerns. These topics include personal safety, online safety, and antibullying.

PACER's National Bullying Prevention Center
www.pacer.org/bullying/resources/cyberbullying

The National Bullying Prevention Center's website features information about cyberbullying, its impacts, and how to address it.

StopBullying.gov
www.stopbullying.gov/cyberbullying/what-is-it

This website is run by the US Department of Health and Human Services. It contains information about cyberbullying, including tips for prevention and coping with its effects.

INDEX

INDEX CONTINUED

IMAGE CREDITS

Cover: © MachineHeadz/iStockphoto
5: © jabejon/iStockphoto
7: © Kathy Hutchins/Shutterstock Images
8: © MachineHeadz/iStockphoto
11: © cokada/iStockphoto
13: © Red Line Editorial
14: © fizkes/iStockphoto
17: © SeventyFour/iStockphoto
19: © Marcos Calvo/iStockphoto
25: © blanscape/iStockphoto
29: © Motortion/iStockphoto
33: © Monkey Business Images/Shutterstock Images
34: © polkadot/iStockphoto
38: © Alina555/iStockphoto
41: © Jstone/Shutterstock Images
44: © Wavebreakmedia/iStockphoto
46: © SolStock/iStockphoto
49: © bodnarchuk/iStockphoto
53: © golubovystock/Shutterstock Images
55: © Tero Vesalainen/iStockphoto
57: © Michael Candelori/Shutterstock Images
59: © Torwaisttudio/Shutterstock Images
61: © SpeedKingz/Shutterstock Images
64: © monkeybusinessimages/iStockphoto
67: © Motortion/iStockphoto
68: © Fractal Pictures/Shutterstock Images

ABOUT THE AUTHOR

Marie-Thérèse Miller is the author of nonfiction books for children and teens, including *Managing Responsibilities*, *Understanding Friendship, Feeling Good About You, Dealing with Psychotic Disorders*, and the Many Ways series. Miller earned a PhD in English from St. John's University, where her academic focus was James Thurber and humor. She and her husband, John, have five children and a grandson.